A **Llama** in the **Family**

BY JOHANNA HURWITZ

Make Room for Elisa
Much Ado About Aldo
New Neighbors for Nora
New Shoes for Silvia
Nora and Mrs. Mind-Your-Own-Business
Once I Was a Plum Tree
Ozzie on His Own
The Rabbi's Girls
Rip-Roaring Russell
Roz and Ozzie
Russell and Elisa
Russell Rides Again
Russell Sprouts
School's Out
School Spirit
Spring Break
Superduper Teddy
Teacher's Pet
Tough-Luck Karen
The Up & Down Spring
A Word to the Wise: And Other Proverbs
Yellow Blue Jay

A Llama in the Family

Johanna Hurwitz

illustrated by Mark Graham

Morrow Junior Books
New York

The author would like to give special thanks to Joy Powell of Green Mountain
Expeditions in Wilmington, Vermont, and Gayle Garrison of West Mountain Farm
in Stamford, Vermont, for sharing information and lore about llamas.

6 7 8 9 10

Library of Congress Cataloging-in-Publication Data
Hurwitz, Johanna.
A llama in the family/Johanna Hurwitz; illustrated by Mark Graham.
p. cm.
Summary: Because Adam hopes that the "big surprise" awaiting him at home has two
wheels and pedals, he is unprepared for the unusual addition to his Vermont family.
ISBN 0-688-13388-6
[1. Llamas—Fiction.   2. Vermont—Fiction.]   I. Graham, Mark, ill.   II. Title.
PZ7.H9574Ll 1994 [Fic]—dc20   94-13612   CIP AC

For Uri,
who brought me to Dilmun.

CONTENTS

❑ ❑ ❑ ❑ ❑

1

A Thursday Surprise

It was the first Thursday in May. I was sitting at the table chewing on a piece of banana that my mother had sliced into my cornflakes for breakfast. I was half awake and half asleep, so I only half heard her when she spoke.

"There may be a big surprise when you get home from school," she said.

"Okay," I answered, swallowing the food in my mouth.

"You shouldn't have said anything, Laura," my father complained. "He'll be disappointed if it doesn't come today."

"What are you talking about?" I asked. I was wide-awake now.

"Oh, nothing," my mother answered. "Forget what I said."

That's the craziest thing I ever heard. "How can I forget about a surprise?" I asked.

"Think about your cornflakes," my father suggested. But who wants to think about cornflakes? I thought about surprises. It wasn't my birthday. That was over and done with last month. I had turned ten. I'd been begging for a new bike, but I hadn't gotten one in December or on my birthday. Could they have ordered one for me now?

"Better hurry," my mother said, interrupting my thoughts. "You don't want to miss the bus."

If I missed the bus, I'd have to ride my rusty old bike to school. I grabbed my lunch bag and stuffed it into my backpack. Tomorrow, I thought excitedly, when I had the new bike, I'd ride it to school, even if I didn't miss the bus. I'd want to show it off to everyone. I wondered what color it would be.

"See you!" I shouted to my parents. My little sister, April, was just coming into the kitchen in her pajamas. Since she doesn't go to school yet, she doesn't get dressed until she's good and ready.

She took her thumb out of her mouth. "Bye, Adam," she called to me. Then she stuck her thumb back where it had come from.

When I got on the school bus, I sat down next to my friend Justin. We almost always sit together.

"Hi," he greeted me.

"Hi," I said back to him. "Guess what?" I said, wanting to share my good news with him. "I'm getting a new bike today."

Justin knew that I'd been disappointed not to get one like his on my birthday.

"How come?" he asked, sounding surprised. "It's not a special occasion or anything."

"I know. But you can get presents even when it isn't your birthday." Then I remembered what my father had said. "I'm pretty sure I'm getting it today. But if it isn't today, it will probably be tomorrow."

Justin nodded his head. "Did you study your spelling?" he asked. I saw he had his notebook open.

I'd gone over the words at home and was positive I knew them all. So while Justin studied, I looked out the window.

I live in Vermont, and it's very beautiful in May. The snow is finally gone from the sides of the roads, with only the tiniest bit still up on the ski trails on the mountains. The mud has dried up and the trees and fields are just turning green after the winter. But I wasn't admiring the view that morning.

And although I aced the spelling quiz we had before lunch, I didn't spend much time thinking about schoolwork either. I kept waiting for the day to be over and for my new bike. I just wanted to jump on it and take a long ride.

When school finally ended, and the bus dropped me at my stop, I ran the last part of the way along the dirt road. As I reached the wood fence surrounding our property, I thought I should act cool. I should pretend that my mother hadn't slipped and mentioned anything at breakfast. I should act surprised. So I slowed down and walked rather than ran toward our house.

"Hi, Mom," I shouted when I saw her walking across the yard. "I'm home."

April came running toward me. "Adam. Adam. Come and see," she yelled. "You'll never believe it."

At that moment I felt so happy. I knew my bike had arrived. This really was the day. But I remembered to keep calm. "What is it, April?" I asked, pretending I didn't know. I'd let her have the thrill of showing me the bicycle. I took off my backpack and threw it on the porch. Then I followed April.

She grabbed me by the arm and took me around the back of the house. I thought the bicycle must be in the stable. But standing outside our stable was one of the weirdest animals I'd ever seen. I stopped in amazement. It wasn't a horse or a sheep. It looked a little bit familiar. Maybe I'd seen one when we visited the Washington Zoo a few years ago. Or maybe I'd seen a picture of one in a book at school.

I turned to my mother, who had joined us. "Is it ours?" I asked, bewildered. Nothing like this had ever been on our property before.

My mother nodded her head as she patted the hairy back of the creature.

"Yes. Yes. Yes," cried April, jumping up and down.

"What is it?"

"A llama!" April shouted. She was so proud to know something I didn't.

"Where did it come from?" It couldn't have just walked across a field. I'd never seen any llamas around here.

"On a truck. When you were at school."

I went closer to investigate the strange creature. It was white with a dark patch on its rump. It wasn't as tall as I am, but it had a long neck, so I had to look up to see its head. I looked at the big black eyes that looked back at me with a sad expression. In a way, the long neck reminded me of the camels I had seen at the zoo. But the llama didn't have any humps. It turned away from me and chewed on the grass near its feet.

"Llamas usually live in South America, in Peru," my mother said. "Their hair is used to make wool and they are good at carrying things."

"What are we going to do with this one?" I wondered aloud. My mother doesn't even like to sew buttons, so I couldn't imagine her making wool. And my father has a pickup truck, so I didn't think we needed the llama to carry stuff.

"I have a plan," my mother said. "I've been thinking about starting a business for a long time. I'm going to advertise that people can go on a hike with the llama. I'll pack a lunch for them, and they can

6 ❏

have their pictures taken with the llama too. I think tourists will love it. They're always looking for something new to do when they come here on their vacations."

As she spoke, I tried going up to the llama. But it kept walking a few steps away from me. I guess it was afraid of me or shy. My mother took hold of the halter around the llama's head so it couldn't move. "Here," she said. "Feel."

The llama's back felt like my head when I need a haircut. It was covered with a thick coat of long hair. It wasn't like the tight curly hair on Mr. Harris's sheep. Mr. Harris lives a couple of miles from here, and he has two dozen sheep. I wondered what he would say when he saw this new animal of ours.

"I've been thinking about a good name for him," my mother said. That's when I found out this llama was a boy.

"Snowie or Woolly?" I suggested. That's what he was, white and woolly.

"No. A Vermont llama should have a Vermont name. I think we should name him Ethan Allen. What do you think of that?"

I'd learned about Ethan Allen at school. He fought in the Revolutionary War as the leader of a troop of brave men called the Green Mountain Boys. He had a brother named Ira who fought with him. There's a motel about twenty miles from here named after

Ethan Allen. And I've seen ads for furniture named after him too. I bet if he could know about it, he'd be very surprised that all those things, and now a llama, were given his name.

"Can you say Ethan Allen?" my mother asked April.

"E-N-L-N," echoed April. She has trouble saying some words.

I laughed at her funny pronunciation. Even though she is almost four years old, some words seem to get stuck in her mouth and don't come out the right way.

"Hiya, Ethan Allen," I called to the llama.

He backed away from me again.

"I have a treat for him," my mother said. "If you give it to him a couple of times, I don't think he'll be afraid of you anymore."

April and I followed her into the stable. She opened a huge sack and poured something from it into a pail. "It's cold rolled oats," my mother said.

It looked like uncooked oatmeal. I picked out one little piece and tasted it. "Blah," I said. "What kind of treat is this?" It was like putting a small piece of paper in my mouth.

"Perfect for a llama," my mother said, laughing. "Watch."

She gave me the pail and Ethan Allen came right over. He stuck his head inside and didn't take it out again until there was nothing left inside the pail but the inside of the pail. Imagine eating such a strange, dry snack and *liking* it.

I had two pages of arithmetic homework to do, and twice, in between problems, I got up and went outside to take another look at Ethan Allen. I still couldn't believe that we had such an unusual animal in our yard. Both times he was minding his own business and eating the grass along the side of the stable. If he kept that up, we wouldn't have to worry about mowing it anymore.

When supper was over, I went outside once more to check on the llama. My dad had put him inside the stable for the night. We'd always had the stable. It came with our house. The people who lived here before us had a couple of horses. When my friends come over, the stable is a great place to play hide-and-seek. But this was the first time my family had had an animal to sleep inside it.

I wondered if Ethan Allen would get lonely in the stable all by himself in the dark. Maybe he'd miss his mother, wherever she was. I wouldn't want to spend the whole night in there. I tried to pat him on the back, but he stepped as far away from me as he could. He was still feeling shy, I guess.

I looked him up and down very carefully, from his long pointed ears to his two-toed feet. His ears were a little like a rabbit's and his feet were like a deer's.

❏ 9

For such a large animal, he had a small, stubby bit of a tail. He was certainly a strange creature. Before, he had been silent. Now he was making a sort of humming sound, as if he were talking to himself.

"Don't be scared, Ethan," I whispered to him. "You'll be safe in here. I'll come and see you in the morning." He turned and looked at me as I spoke. His eyes behind their long white lashes looked sadder than ever.

"You're going to like it here. I promise," I whispered. I reached out, and this time I managed to pat his hairy flank. "I'll be your friend," I told him. He didn't make a sound. He just kept looking at me and chewing his cud, the way a cow does.

"Adam," my mother called from the door of the house. "It's time for your bath."

"Sleep tight," I told Ethan Allen. I wondered if he would sleep standing up, like a horse, or if he would lie down during the night.

"Adam Fine," my mother called again.

"I gotta go," I said. "See you in the morning."

It wasn't until I was bathed and lying in bed that evening that I suddenly realized something. The surprise hadn't been a bicycle after all. I felt cheated and disappointed. I was still stuck with my old one that had once belonged to my cousin Ted. It had thin tires and lots of rust. It had been worn when I got it and now it was worse. My father said it was my fault because I had left the bike out in the rain.

I'd been so sure that I was going to finally get a new bike today. Now I'd have to tell Justin that I'd been wrong. I wished I hadn't said anything about it on the bus.

And yet even though I still wanted a mountain bike, I realized that I wasn't completely unhappy. It would be fun to go to school tomorrow and tell all my friends about Ethan Allen. None of them had a llama in their family.

2

Ethan Allen
Goes to School

❏ ❏ ❏ ❏ ❏ ❏ ❏ ❏ ❏ ❏

I guess I shouldn't have been surprised that my mother went out and bought a llama. She's crazy about all animals. Once when I was at Justin's house, a mouse ran across the kitchen floor. Mrs. Rice let out such a scream that I became terrified. I thought something really dreadful had happened. So I screamed too. And that made Justin scream. Imagine three people yelling and jumping about a kitchen as if something ghastly had happened. All because the sight of one tiny mouse had frightened Justin's mom.

Not my mother. When she saw a mouse in our kitchen last winter, she said, "Oh, the darling. I bet he's hungry." She rushed to throw a piece of bread onto the floor for the mouse to eat. Instead, the mouse got frightened of my mother and ran away. My mom wanted to leave scraps of bread and cheese all around the house so he could have a quiet feast at night when we were asleep. But my dad put his foot down. "Mice do not belong inside the house," he said.

"You're right," my mom agreed. "How do you feel about adopting one of Eileen's kittens?" Eileen is my mother's friend, and her cat had just had a new litter. Every few months that cat has a litter and each time my mother suggests taking one of the kittens. She thought the smell of a cat in the house would keep mice away. "Not this time," my father always says. He said it again last winter.

So my mother went out and bought humane mousetraps. Justin, April, and I watched as she baited the little plastic traps with peanut butter. Chunky. She put four of them around the kitchen, and the next morning two of the traps contained tiny mice. They sure must love peanut butter. My dad thought she should flush them down the toilet.

"Can they swim?" April asked as she peeked into the traps. She wasn't afraid of the mice at all.

"Why did I get a humane trap?" asked my mom. "Not so the mice could go swimming in the middle of the winter." She took the traps and emptied them inside the shed.

"They'll be back," my dad predicted.

"Goody," said April.

"Are you sure you don't want a kitten?" my mom asked again. In the end, she used up half a jar of peanut butter and she caught nine tiny mice. And, in the end, my dad gave in. Now we have a calico kitten named Molly Stark. That's another Vermont name. The first Molly Stark's husband was in the Revolutionary War. He wrote her a letter saying that his company needed men. So she recruited all the men in the area and brought them herself to the camp where the soldiers were stationed.

Since the arrival of our Molly Stark, we haven't seen any more mice. Besides mice and cats, my mom loves deer. She doesn't even mind when they come and eat our flowers in the spring. They ate the tulips that she was growing. And when she planted a whole bunch of other stuff, like hyacinths, anemones, and gladiolas, the deer ate them too. Anyone else would have had a fit. But not my mom.

"Deer need to eat too," she said. I guess she feels that offering them bulbs of so many different flowers gives them a balanced diet.

So now I know that besides mice, cats, and deer, my mother also likes llamas.

"A llama?" said Justin when I told him the news. "What good is that? Can you ride him? I'm getting a horse as soon as school is out."

"Really?" I asked. I thought maybe he was just making it up.

"Yep. You'll see," Justin promised.

If it was true, it wasn't fair. Justin has a new mountain bike and a dog *and* his own computer. Mr. Rice, his father, is a lawyer who makes big money.

"The world needs all sorts of people," my dad explained to me when I was little and asked him what a lawyer was. My father has a store that sells carpeting and linoleum. I could understand that because I can see the store and what he has in it. When I went with Justin to his father's office, all I saw was a big desk with a lot of papers on it. No one would want to buy them, I thought. But my dad explained that those papers were deeds to properties and contracts and other important things.

Mr. Rice even helped my mom when she set up her new business: Fine Llama Treks. She had to be licensed by the National Park Service, and she needed permission from the power company to use their land for her treks. I wouldn't have guessed starting a new business could be so complicated.

"If this thing takes off and I make some money, I'm going to buy you a new bike," my mother promised. She must have read my mind. Even though I was growing fond of our pet llama, I still wanted that bike.

As pets go, a llama is pretty weird. Ethan Allen didn't pay much attention to us or make much noise. But every once in a while, he would hum to himself a bit. I didn't know if he was complaining or if he was happy. I couldn't understand llama talk.

He didn't follow me around the way a dog would.

And even though I could ride him, it wasn't like riding a horse. I would sit on his back, without a saddle, holding on to his long hair. Then if I was lucky, he would walk slowly about the yard. Sometimes, he just stood still. Mostly he ignored us, and he almost looked like a statue until he blinked his eyes. Then he would suddenly lower his head and eat some grass or leaves. Maybe he was very hungry. Or maybe he was homesick for Peru, I thought. Then I remembered that he was a Vermont llama. He'd never been to Peru. I didn't know how he felt about living with us.

"I'm glad I'm getting a horse and not a llama," said Justin when he first saw me sitting on Ethan Allen.

"Anybody can have a horse. Thousands of people do. Who else do you know who has a llama?" I asked, defending this new member of the Fine family and wishing he was a bike at the same time.

"Who else would want a llama?" asked Justin.

Nevertheless, he climbed up onto Ethan Allen's back when I got off. "Can't he go any faster?" he asked as the llama moved very slowly across the yard.

"Nope," I answered. "He's not a racehorse. He's a pack animal and he can carry heavy weights, like you."

Justin isn't fat. He's only a little bigger than me, so he's a whole lot less than a hundred pounds, which

16 ❑

my mom said is the limit for a llama. Still, he didn't like my teasing. He kicked Ethan Allen in the ribs.

"Come on. Move," he demanded.

Ethan Allen surprised us both by doing something he had never done before. He turned his head and spat at Justin. It wasn't just any old spit, either. It had a really bad smell. Justin jumped off Ethan Allen one-two-three. And I just stood there laughing. It served Justin right.

After Justin went home, I got the sack of cold rolled oats and put some in the pail. Ethan Allen had been lying on the ground in the funny way he does, with both his front legs under him. When he saw the pail of oats, he jumped right up and came over to me. He stuck his head inside the pail. I combed my fingers through his white hairy back while he ate.

Besides spitting, the only trick Ethan Allen could seem to do was eat his favorite snack from the pail I held out to him. As tricks go, it wasn't much. It was just as well I hadn't shown it to Justin. I knew he wouldn't have been impressed.

Even though Justin didn't think much of our llama, a lot of the kids at school were curious about him. So I got an idea. I asked my teacher, Mrs. Bayles, if I could bring the llama to school. That way everyone could see him.

"What a splendid plan," Mrs. Bayles said. "Of

❑ 17

course, you'll have to tell us all about the llama—where it comes from, what it eats. It will be a combined geography and zoology lesson. Then everyone can sketch pictures of him. That will be like an art lesson." Mrs. Bayles was big on incorporating everything into the school curriculum. I was just thankful she didn't ask me to sing a llama song too. That would have been like a music lesson.

So, one sunny Thursday afternoon in June, my mother drove over in our pickup truck with Ethan Allen in the back. I had already given my llama talk, telling the class that llamas were great animals because they ate only one-third as much as horses. They are like camels in that they don't need to drink much water either. A half gallon of water is all they need for a day.

I explained that a full-grown llama weighs three hundred to four hundred pounds and can carry one-hundred-pound loads. They are surefooted on mountain trails. (Sort of like a mountain bike with four feet, I thought to myself.)

"Are there any questions?" Mrs. Bayles asked the kids in my class.

"How much do llamas cost?" Rick Sanders wanted to know.

I knew the answer to that because I'd asked my parents the same thing. "Males cost between $800 and $2,500," I replied. "And females cost between $5,000 and $10,000."

All the girls in the class burst into applause when they heard that. The boys booed.

"All right, everyone. Calm down. Calm down," Mrs. Bayles said in a stern voice. "Adam. Tell us why there is such a difference in the price."

I felt very embarrassed explaining that females cost more because they can have baby llamas. Then I said that originally llamas came from South America. "The Spaniards, who had never seen them until they explored South America, called them the little camels of the Andes." I had looked this all up in the encyclopedia in our school library. "The Andes are a mountain range in South America where llamas are found."

"So where did you find your llama?" Kitty Grady asked.

"Nowadays, people are breeding llamas in other places. There are llama farms out west in Montana, Colorado, and places like that," I answered. "Now even people in other parts of Vermont are breeding them. My mother got our llama from some people who used to have a pair of them as pets. One died, so the people decided to sell the other. Our llama was born in Vermont," I added proudly. "That's why we named him Ethan Allen."

As I said that, I realized that now Mrs. Bayles was going to want to talk about the Revolutionary War leader. That way, she would have a history lesson too.

Luckily, however, my mother arrived just at that moment. The whole class went out into the school yard to meet Ethan Allen. "Bring your sketchbooks," Mrs. Bayles reminded everyone.

My mother lowered the back of the pickup truck. She kept a wide plank of wood in it, and Ethan Allen used the wood like a ramp to get up and down. I ran up to the truck and took the rope that was attached to his halter and led him down. We had groomed him the day before and his white hair looked smooth, thick, and handsome.

Ethan Allen looked around at all my classmates. I don't think he had ever seen so many people at once. There were twenty-four kids all standing about looking at him. He moved his head around and made one of his funny hums.

A few of the kids came forward to touch him. The llama backed away as Ryan tried to make a grab.

"Sometimes he's a little shy," I said. I was proud that Ethan Allen wasn't afraid of me any longer. "But if you keep your hands behind your back, he'll see that you aren't going to hurt him. Then he'll let you come closer to him."

"He's chewing his cud," observed Kitty. "Just like a cow."

"He looks kind of dumb to me," said Ryan.

"All right, everyone. Open your sketchbooks and draw a picture of the llama," said Mrs. Bayles, ignoring Ryan's comment.

"Me too?" I asked.

"Of course," she said. "You're part of this class, aren't you?"

I dropped the rope that I was holding and started back into the school building. I'd been so excited about showing off Ethan Allen that I hadn't brought my sketchbook outside with me.

"Look," one of the girls in my class called out. "The llama is following Adam."

Sure enough, Ethan Allen had walked across the school yard toward the door, following me.

Ryan, who had never before in his life been known to recite poetry, called out: *Adam had a little llama. Its fleece was white as snow. And everywhere that Adam went, that llama was sure to go.*

Everyone laughed, which made me angry. "You're just jealous," I shouted to Ryan. The words came out of my mouth automatically. Yet somehow, I knew I was 100 percent correct.

3
Lunch with a Llama

❏ ❏ ❏ ❏ ❏ ❏ ❏ ❏ ❏ ❏

My mother placed an advertisement for her llama trips in our local newspaper. It gave the price and our phone number. There was a little drawing of a llama at the top of the ad. I made one and so did my mother. Even April tried to draw a picture of Ethan Allen. We were all surprised when my father made the one that came out the best. Mrs. Bayles would have been proud of his sketch. None of us knew he could draw that well. Neither did he.

"I guess I have a new career," he said when we were admiring the ad.

After that we waited to see if anyone would call to make a reservation. I used to come home from school and ask what I could have for a snack. Now that we had the llama, I would enter the house and say, "Did anyone call about the llama walks today?"

"Not yet," my mom would answer as she handed

me an apple or a couple of cookies and a glass of milk.

Molly Stark would come and rub against my leg as I sat eating at the kitchen table. "What if nobody wants to have lunch with our llama?" I asked. "Will you have to get rid of Ethan Allen?"

My mother shrugged. "I hope not," she said.

While she waited, she kept prepared. She practiced putting a soft saddle with saddlebags on Ethan Allen's back. She had a small portable scale so she could weigh each of the bags and have them properly balanced. When she took him off on a trek, the bags would hold the food, a large picnic blanket, her Polaroid camera, and film.

She also kept Ethan Allen groomed by brushing his hair with a funny brush that had wire bristles. "The more we groom him, the more he will get used to us," my mother said. That made me want to help her. Even Justin liked to come over to my house to help. I had let him feed Ethan Allen a portion of his special cold rolled oats, and when the llama didn't spit at him again, they became friends.

Once, when there hadn't been any rain for many days and Ethan Allen was all dusty from rolling on the ground, Justin and I took the portable vacuum cleaner outside and sucked the dust out of his long hair.

"I'd rather shampoo myself this way, any day,"

said Justin. "What about you?" He pointed the vacuum cleaner at my scalp. Then I grabbed it and gave him a vacuum shampoo while Ethan Allen stood by, humming and watching us fooling around.

Sure enough, the more time I spent with the llama, the friendlier he became. He seemed really curious about me, just as I was curious about him. After a bit, I discovered that if I stood real still and kept my hands at my sides, he'd walk over to me and put his nose right up to my nose.

"He's kissing you!" April shouted in amazement. "Will he kiss me?"

But April couldn't stand still long enough for a kiss. Whenever Ethan Allen approached her she began giggling and jumping up and down with excitement.

"I think the llama is bonding with you, Adam," my mother said.

"What does that mean?" I asked.

"It means he feels close to you, almost as if you were his mother or another llama."

I thought that was very funny, and I tried to imitate the humming sound of a llama. Maybe I could learn to talk to him.

"If Ethan Allen thinks you're a llama, it means you need a haircut," said Justin. I think he was a little hurt that Ethan Allen hadn't gotten around to kissing him yet.

For a while, it looked as if no one was ever going to respond to the newspaper ad.

"Maybe the advertisement needs to be re-designed," suggested my dad. I guess he felt bad since it was his drawing in the ad and no one seemed to notice it.

"It's still early. Summer hasn't even officially begun," my mom reminded him. She sounded calm, but I'm sure she was anxious. She had wanted to start a business, but so far all she had was a llama and an ad.

So we were all excited when Mom got her first reservation to go out with the llama. Two couples traveling together in our area called. The arrangements were made. The sandwiches were made (Vermont cheddar cheese and tomato on homemade whole-wheat bread). And off they went. I was sorry that I missed it all because I was still in school. April was at her play group, and when that was over for the day, my father picked her up and she spent the rest of the time with him in his store. She likes to play with scraps of carpet.

Mom told us all about the experience when we were eating supper.

"They didn't need my camera. They used up two rolls of their own film," she said. "Ethan Allen was wonderful. He held still when they posed next to him."

26 ❏

"That's what he does best," I said. "Standing still."

"Did they like their lunch?" Dad asked.

"They loved it. They asked me where they could buy some cheese to take home. But I think that I'm going to bring something fancier next time. I'm going to pack some salads in plastic containers, and I'll bring a thermos filled with my cold blueberry soup."

"Oh, those lucky people," I said. I love my mom's blueberry soup.

"What about Ethan Allen? Did he have a good time?" April wanted to know.

"It's hard to say. He can't tell me."

"Can I come along on one of your treks?" I asked.

"Sure. When school is out. That is, if I get more customers," Mom said. But having gotten one group of customers, we were all feeling confident that there would be others.

So then I had two reasons to be eager for the last day of school. I was looking forward to vacation time, and I was also curious to have a chance to see how Fine Llama Treks worked.

School ended on June 24. And by good luck, my mother had five people signed up for a trek the very next day. April was unhappy that she couldn't go along. But there was no way she would be able to walk three miles. Ethan Allen would already be burdened with the food, so he wouldn't be able to carry her also.

Mom and I and Ethan Allen met the customers in front of the post office. I led Ethan Allen out of the pickup truck and my mom parked the truck in the back. I helped her attach the bags to the llama's saddle. Then I stood holding his rope and feeling very important as we waited. A couple of people I know from town came out of the post office to admire Ethan Allen. I guess if I had a cow or a dog at the end of the rope, they would have come over too. But a llama holding his head in its proud way is certainly a striking sight. I noticed several cars slowed down as they passed by.

In a few minutes, everyone was there. My mother explained that we'd be going down the dirt road in back of the post office that leads toward McLean's farm. The McLean family owns about a hundred acres of land, and they gave my mother permission to use their trails. Their land is adjacent to land owned by the power company, and we had permission to use that land too. In winter, a lot of people use the trails for cross-country skiing.

All the people on the trek were very curious about our llama. I was interested in them. What kind of people wanted to spend three hours walking in the woods with a woman they didn't know and a type of animal they'd hardly ever seen before? Most of the

hikers had gray or white hair, so I guess they were very old.

They all took turns holding the rope attached to Ethan Allen's halter. It occurred to me that if we had a pair of llamas, each person could have had a longer turn and the two llamas could have shared the load in the saddlebags. It also would be more exciting to see two llamas walking through the woods. But I remembered how expensive a llama was, so I doubted that Mom would be in a hurry to purchase a second one.

As we walked along, Mom talked about the various wildflowers we saw. She pointed out a red-headed woodpecker, and a little later we saw a hawk. "There's probably a nest with baby birds in it that he's watching," Mom said.

"You mean he's the father?" asked one of the women.

"No. Unfortunately, I mean he's checking out his lunch menu," my mother explained.

"Oh, that's awful," said the woman.

"It isn't a happy thought, but that's the law of nature. Did you notice these rocks?" my mother asked, pointing in another direction and trying to distract the woman from her thoughts of the hawk.

I was impressed with how much my mother knew about the woods. She went to college and got a degree in earth science, and she's been teaching me about things since I was a little kid. But I'd been taking it for granted. Listening to her explain things to the people on the trek reminded me of just how much she knew.

Because there were so many people and the trail was so narrow, and also because Ethan Allen can't be rushed, it took about an hour just to cover a mile and a half. Finally, we reached the spot my mother had selected for the picnic. It looked out on Lake Whitingham, and there were trees for shade. It was a good spot.

I helped her tie Ethan Allen's rope to a tree using a slip knot. Then we removed the saddlebags with all the food.

There were sandwiches of smoked turkey, tomato and cucumber salad, a big thermos filled with blueberry soup (my mother used frozen berries, since the fresh ones wouldn't be ripe for at least another month).

"Can you fill everyone's cups?" she asked me.

"Sure," I said, taking the thermos from her.

I poured a cup of blueberry soup for one of the ladies, and my mother followed me with a container of vanilla yogurt, which tastes great in the soup.

As I moved toward the second woman, who was holding her cup out, I tripped on a rock. The good news is that I didn't spill very much of the soup on the woman. The bad news is that I spilled the rest of it on the ground.

"There are a lot of other things to eat," my mother said quickly. I was sure she would have something else to say when we got home.

"I have iced tea and fruit juice. Which would you like?" she asked everyone. "There are homemade chocolate-chip cookies too."

The only other calamity of the day was the arrival of the blackflies. Unlike mosquitoes, blackflies don't buzz in your ears and warn you of their presence. They just attack silently and are especially good at biting behind your ears or under your chin. Blackflies are part of June in Vermont, but they disappear by the Fourth of July. Maybe the reason people shoot off firecrackers is to celebrate the end of blackflies.

The flies attacked us as we were walking back to our starting point. Luckily, my mother was prepared for everything. She pulled out a large bottle of insect repellent and passed it around. Soon we had rubbed the liquid on the exposed parts of our bodies. I guess if I had to spill something, it was better that I spilled the soup than the insect repellent.

All the people had their pictures taken standing next to Ethan Allen and thanked my mother for a wonderful time. Except for my embarrassment about spilling the soup, it was kind of fun. But I don't think I'd want to do it over and over, the way Mom and Ethan Allen would be doing all summer long.

Mom took the money that each of the people paid her.

At supper that night, I suddenly remembered. "Hey. Now you've had a total of nine customers. Did you make enough money yet to buy me a bike?" I asked.

"Whoa, there," Dad said. "I thought you were better in arithmetic than that. Nine people taking llama treks have paid for less than one leg on that animal. You can't think about a new bike before that llama is paid for. And what about the ads?"

"What about them?" I asked.

"They have to be paid for too. To say nothing of the sandwiches, salads, and blueberry soup ingredients. And don't forget the cold rolled oats that Ethan Allen likes to snack on," he added.

"Oh," I said, disappointed. It made me think that by the time my mom made enough money to buy me a new bike, I'd probably be a grown man with a job and no time to go bike riding.

It started me thinking. What could I possibly do on my own to speed up the purchase of that mountain bike?

4

April's Birthday

❏ ❏ ❏ ❏ ❏ ❏ ❏ ❏ ❏ ❏

People usually expect that a person named April was born in April. But Mom just loved the name, and when she couldn't use it for me, since I'm a boy, it must have stuck in her head. So even when my sister was born in July, that didn't stop my mother.

That was why on Tuesday, July 9, we were celebrating April's fourth birthday. She had invited the little girls in her play group, eight in all, to come to a party at our house. The girls ranged in age from three to five. With a houseful of little kids, I would have liked to have spent the day away from home, with my friends. But my mom offered to give me an extra slice of birthday cake and to pay me five dollars if I stayed home and helped her with the party. I probably would have gotten an extra slice of cake anyhow, but the five dollars was very tempting.

"Could Justin come and help me help you?" I asked. "Eight little girls is a lot of little girls."

"Okay," my mother agreed. "I'll pay him too. But you guys have got to promise not to fool around. I'm really counting on you to give me a hand."

I promised. After all, in addition to the five dollars, this was a good chance to prove how responsible I was becoming.

Luckily, the weather on July 9 was perfect. It wasn't too hot, even though the sun was out. It wasn't too cold, even though there was a little breeze. The blackflies were gone, and the mosquitoes must have been out of town for the day. It was just perfect.

The plan for the party was to let each of the girls have a turn sitting on Ethan Allen. I would hold his halter and take them for a walk around the yard. Then Mom would use her Polaroid camera, and each girl would get her picture taken with our llama as a souvenir. When they weren't riding on Ethan Allen, the girls could play in the sandbox or on the swing set that my dad built. It has a swing made out of an old inner tube, a slide, and a climbing section.

"Lunch will take up a lot of time," Mom promised Justin and me. "You just see that no one gets hurt or does anything foolish." She was busy putting a cloth on the old redwood table that we have out in the yard. She was going to make hamburgers and hot dogs on the barbecue grill. There was a big pot of baked beans, and there were potato chips and lemonade too.

"Look at my cake!" said April. She took her thumb out of her mouth and pointed to the cake that Mom had baked the night before. It was chocolate with chocolate frosting. Mom placed it in the center of the table. It looked fantastic, and it took all my self-control not to put out my finger and get a little swipe of the frosting.

"I could eat that whole cake myself," Justin told April. But he grinned when he said it, and she knew he was just teasing her.

Even Ethan Allen walked over to the picnic table. He must have been aware that something out of the ordinary was about to happen. He stood looking around him in a way that showed his curiosity. I bet he had never seen a birthday cake before because he stared at it for a long time.

"Four-year-old girls hardly ever suck their thumbs," my mother reminded April.

"I forgot," said April. She was trying hard to stop, but her thumb kept getting into her mouth.

"What's your favorite present so far?" I asked her. I knew she really liked the one I gave her. It was a red wagon, almost new. I paid only two dollars for it at the flea market we have in town every Saturday and Sunday from May through October. Justin and I spend a lot of time there. Many of the dealers who come bring real old junk that you'd have to be nuts to buy. Luckily for them, there are a lot of tourists who go wild for dusty old books, musty old rugs, and rusty old tools.

But sometimes we find great stuff. Justin has a collection of unusual old keys. They don't open anything, but they sure look neat. I've gotten very good at bargaining with the dealers. If they say something costs five dollars, I can almost always talk them into reducing the price to half that amount. Once I even sold a carton of old bottles that I found in our attic to one of the dealers. My dad says I'll probably make a great businessman someday.

I usually get presents for people at the flea market. For Mother's Day, I gave my mom a ceramic vase that had only a tiny chip in the top. No one would ever guess that I paid just fifty cents for it. When I filled the vase with water and some wildflowers that I had picked, the chip didn't show at all. Mom loved it, and April loved her wagon. She had spent half the morning taking poor Molly Stark for rides in it.

I kept hoping that maybe by a miracle, someday someone would be selling an almost-new mountain bike for a price I could afford. But I knew that was crazy. An almost-new bike would cost nearly as much as a brand-new one. Still, I kept watching and hoping.

It wasn't long before April's guests arrived and Molly Stark was free to go sleep in the sun. The wagon was filled with the presents that everyone brought. April pulled the wagon proudly toward the picnic table. Justin and I helped her over the biggest bumps in the yard.

"You can open the presents at lunchtime," Mom said. "Now, let's have the rides. Who wants to be first?" she asked as we approached Ethan Allen.

I thought all the kids would be jumping around and fighting about who would have the first turn. But I was wrong. Three of the smallest girls were afraid to go up on his back. Even the bigger girls seemed reluctant.

"I want to ride in the red wagon," said a little girl named Corey.

"Me too. Me too," all the other girls copied.

So April took all the gift-wrapped packages out of the wagon, and I put them on the table. Then I found myself pulling first one girl and then another across the yard in the red wagon. It wasn't easy. If I had known that was going to happen, I would have thought twice about buying the wagon for April. Still, I was glad the birthday present I gave my sister was such a hit. And I was even more glad that I had Justin there to give me a hand.

We were in for a big surprise when we finally went over to the picnic table. There was Ethan Allen, his white face covered with chocolate frosting. The cake, which had been left on the table, looked awful, and Ethan looked awful funny. But I can't say that I blamed him. He'd been eating grass and leaves and

pine needles with only those boring cold rolled oats for an occasional treat for several weeks now. I guess he wanted a real treat!

"Oh, Ethan!" my mother gasped. All the little kids began laughing and shouting. Sticking their faces in a chocolate-frosted cake is just the sort of thing they would have liked to do. Ethan Allen just looked around at everyone with his big black eyes and hummed a bit. If a llama could smile, I think he would have been smiling.

I grabbed a paper napkin and wiped some of the chocolate off his face.

"Shoo. Shoo," my mother said to him. I guess she was worried that he would try to eat more of the party food. Justin and I walked with him over toward the stable. And I filled a pail with rolled oats as a distraction for him.

Back at the picnic table, the charcoal was ready, and while April opened her presents and all the little girls sat around watching her, Mom put the hamburgers on to cook. Soon the ground was covered with wrapping paper, and there was a pile of games and puzzles and a couple of books for us to read to April. The air was filled with a good smell from the hamburgers.

Justin and I helped serve, and then we each ate two hamburgers and a hot dog with all the fixings.

There was no cake, but there was still ice cream.

And Mom stuck five candles into April's portion—four for her age and one to grow on. April closed her eyes when she blew out the candles and then promptly announced in a proud voice, "I wished I wouldn't suck my thumb anymore."

Of course, you're not supposed to tell what you wish if you want it to come true. So I guess April will keep on with her thumb in her mouth—at least for a while longer.

The girls played tag and chased each other around on the grass. Justin went off for a moment to see where Ethan Allen had wandered. A minute later, Justin came running toward me. "This is something you've got to see," he shouted. So I followed Justin, and he led me to the swing set. There was Ethan Allen with his head stuck inside the inner-tube swing. For the second time that day, I thought he might be trying to smile at us. Like sticking his head in the birthday cake, this was something he had never done before.

Meanwhile, my mother and all of April's friends had come running over. The kids cheered and clapped their hands. They thought that Ethan Allen had put his head through the inner tube just to entertain them. And I think they were right. My mother ran and got her camera and took his picture. Then Justin and I tried to pull him out. I got the idea of letting the air out of the tube, and then it was easy.

❑ 41

The kids all cheered again when Ethan Allen was free.

"I want to ride him now," said Corey. And, of course, just like before, everyone shouted, "Me too. Me too." What a bunch of copycats!

Luckily, Mom said it was too late for rides. Thank goodness for that because I don't think I would have had the energy to take all of them around the yard, even with Justin to help. And I don't think Ethan Allen would have wanted to do it either. He'd had enough excitement for one day.

But we posed the little girls, one at a time, standing next to the llama. All of the girls were holding their pictures when their mothers drove up to take them home.

April's red wagon came in handy. Justin and I loaded all the dirty dishes in it and pulled them into the house. When my dad phoned from the store to find out how the party had gone, Mom reported on Ethan Allen and the cake. So, on his way home from work, he stopped at the bakery. He bought a cake and we put it on the table *inside* the house, where Ethan Allen wouldn't be able to get at it.

That's how I got my two slices after all. In the evening, Mom got two different phone calls from people about booking her and Ethan Allen for a Fine Llama Trek. Both calls came from parents of little girls who had been at the party. Each family was expecting out-of-town visitors. When they saw their daughters' snapshots with our llama, it reminded them of this new form of entertainment for their guests.

So everyone was happy with the way the day turned out. But watching April sitting on the floor and playing with her birthday toys made me think some more about the present I had wanted and not gotten on my birthday. I put my five dollars in my bank. I was glad to have it, but it wouldn't pay for even a pedal on that mountain bike.

5

Looking for April

❑ ❑ ❑ ❑ ❑ ❑ ❑ ❑ ❑ ❑

Just after April's birthday, Ethan Allen came up with a new trick. From his point of view, it was the best one yet. We were eating our breakfast, and I heard the familiar sound of his hum. I looked up from my scrambled eggs. There was Ethan Allen, walking right into our kitchen.

"Hey. Look who's here!" I shouted, jumping up from the table. I knocked my glass of orange juice over, but I was so surprised, I didn't even realize it.

Of course, I took the llama outside right away. He must have been disappointed. He thought he'd get to see what life was like inside our house. He'd been looking through the window at us for a couple of weeks. But I never would have guessed that he'd be so interested in us that he'd want to come into the house.

Due to July's hot weather, we left the stable door open at night. Actually, we'd discovered that Ethan

Allen could open it himself anyhow, so there wasn't much point in closing it. But now he was free to go in or out as he wished. And since we have a fence all around our property, it didn't really matter where he slept. Llamas probably spend the nights outdoors in Peru. Even when it rained, it didn't seem to bother Ethan Allen.

He was outside in our yard a couple of weeks earlier when it suddenly started raining. We would have put him inside the stable if we had been home. We'd gone off to Brattleboro to buy some shirts and jeans at the Independence Day sales that some of the stores were running. We drove back in the rain, and the sun was just breaking through the clouds when we got home. There was Ethan Allen calmly eating grass as usual. What was unusual was that he smelled like a wet sweater. I gave him a hug anyhow, and then I had to go into the house and change because my T-shirt got soaking wet from him.

"I bet he gets lonely," I said the morning he walked into our kitchen. "After all, I have loads of friends to hang out with, but Ethan Allen is the only llama for miles around."

My mom looked up from mopping my spilt orange juice. "Ideally, we should have two llamas," she told me. "They are social animals and need another llama to be friends with. But it's too expensive to even think about. That's why it's nice he likes you so much."

"That's why he bonded with me," I reminded her. I shoved the rest of my toast into my mouth and got ready to go off.

Some days, I went down to the school that had been set up for summer as a recreation center. It was an especially good plan on rainy days because they had some neat arts-and-craft supplies, and I'd made some good stuff, including a lanyard woven out of blue and green plastic strips. I wore it around my neck with a whistle on it. I discovered that if I blew my whistle, Ethan Allen would look in my direction. And after a while, when I blew my whistle he would even come toward me and make his funny llama sounds. So without planning it, I had taught him a new trick. From my point of view, it was the best one yet.

On hot, sunny days, I usually met Justin and my other friends, Greg, Doug, and Larry, at the lake. We never got tired of swimming out to the raft and back to the shore. Lots of times, the guys would ride over to my house with me when I was going home. They all liked to visit Ethan Allen. I wished summer would last forever.

The only thing I didn't like about summer was getting to the school or the lake. I had to ride my old bike. If only I had a mountain bike, like most of my friends, riding would be a whole lot easier. Mountain bikes have fat tires with heavy treads that are much better on the bumpy dirt roads we have around here. And the handlebars go straight across, so you can sit much more comfortably when you ride. Vermont has a lot of hills, as well as the mountains for which it's famous. Getting up and down them on my rusty old bike was one big pain. I'd be exhausted by the half-mile ride before I even got halfway to where I was going.

Mom's business was slowly picking up. In a good week, she was taking two or three groups of people out on llama treks. The house always seemed to smell of cinnamon and blueberries because there was always a pot of her special soup cooking. Everyone loved it when she served the soup as part of her lunch menu. In fact, she had had to photocopy a whole pile of her recipes because all her customers wanted to make the soup when they got home. To tell the truth, this was one summer when I'd eaten more than enough of that cold, sweet fruit soup. I'd be glad when the blueberry season was over, and she would cook something else.

Yet even with eight to ten tourists a week going on llama treks, my mom was still paying off the cost of buying Ethan Allen. So a new bike seemed a long way into the future.

Every weekend, I kept checking with the dealers

at the flea market. I didn't announce I was looking for a bike. That's one sure way to drive up a price. But nevertheless, I made the rounds of the place just in case one was on display. I also hit on a new plan.

My mother subscribes to a magazine about New England. Every month I flip through it, looking at the pictures. But one day, I noticed that each issue has a column about what people want to trade for something else. There are all sorts of things people want and all sorts of things they already have that they don't want. The ads are fun to read:

> Will swap old sheet music/music books for authentic Revolutionary War memorabilia.

> Will swap brand-new guitar for antique typewriter.

> Will swap antique gold-plated pocket watch in good condition for collection of old political campaign buttons.

My plan was to keep checking out the ads. Maybe there would be someone who had a new bike to trade for something that we owned. Or if that didn't work, maybe I could find the thing they wanted at the flea market. I'd seen lots of political campaign buttons and old typewriters for sale real cheap. With the five dollars I had earned at April's birthday party and the few other dollars I had in my bank, to say nothing of the bargaining skills I had developed, I might be able to work out some sort of deal. So I kept reading the magazine ads and watching what was for sale at the flea market. I was determined that I would have a new bike before school started in September.

I guess one thing that made me feel a little better about not already having my new bike was that Justin never got a horse. I could have been mean and asked him about it. But if he wanted that horse as much as I wanted a new bike, I knew it would make him feel bad. So I pretended he had never bragged about getting one. I guess that's why we're good friends.

The other thing that made me feel good was Ethan Allen. He'd sure grown on me. I was certain that the expression in his eyes changed when I came up to him. It was hard to believe that once I had needed a pail of his special oats to get him to hold still. Now he let me scratch his hairy back and hug him whenever I wanted. In fact, more and more, he seemed to follow me around the yard. He seemed more curious about things now than he had been when he first came to live with us too. Just the way he walked into our house showed that he was interested. When he first came to us, all he cared about was eating.

One day in late July, I came home from swimming to find my mother calling for April. "I can't find her. I don't know where she is," Mom said, looking very worried.

"She's probably just hiding and wants you to keep looking," I said impatiently. I was exhausted from riding home from the lake. Half an hour ago, my skin had been cool and comfortable. Now I was all hot and sweaty, and I didn't feel like playing hide-and-seek with April.

But after I went into the house, had a cold drink, and splashed water on my face and neck to cool off a bit, I went outside to help search for her after all.

"I don't want to call your father and get him all upset," Mom said. "But it's not like April to wander off. And she doesn't usually hide from me either."

"Maybe she fell asleep somewhere," I said. "You look again inside and I'll look outside. She could be sleeping in her bed or something."

Ten minutes later, April was still missing. Furthermore, I realized that Ethan Allen wasn't around either. They couldn't both be playing hide-and-seek. A terrible thought came to me, and I followed the fence around our property. Sure enough, I discovered that the fence had been knocked down at one place. April and Ethan Allen must have gone off together.

There are a lot of woods nearby to get lost in. And

there was also the possibility that they had gone on the road. I didn't know which was worse, the dense woods or the traffic on the road. Either way, they could be in big trouble. I sure wished we had a dog to help us. They're good at smelling and tracking.

"I have to call the police," my mother said, looking at the downed fence posts that I showed her. Her face looked white and strained. It scared me to see her looking like that.

"I'll keep checking around. I'm sure she just wandered off somewhere nearby," I said, hoping I was right.

I didn't know where to begin in the woods, so I decided to go along the road and stop at our various neighbors'. Just maybe April and Ethan Allen had gone to visit one of them.

So while my mother went back into the house to make the phone call, I grabbed my bike and started down the road. My first stop was at the home of Mr. and Mrs. Cobb. I knew April was a little afraid of the Cobbs' big German shepherd, so she was unlikely to visit them. Still, they were our nearest neighbors, so it made sense to start with them. As I cycled, I thought of April. Wherever she was, she was probably sucking her thumb, I thought.

Lady, the Cobbs' dog, began barking as soon as I approached the house. Mrs. Cobb came out to see what the racket was. "I'm looking for my sister and our llama," I said. "They're missing. Have you seen them?"

"April?" asked Mrs. Cobb. "I haven't seen her since the Fourth of July, when we were all watching the parade. She can't be far. Maybe they just walked down the road into town." She said it matter-of-factly, as if four-year-old girls and llamas walked down the road every day of the week.

"Thanks," I said to Mrs. Cobb, and started off again. I stopped at the end of our dirt road and asked old Mr. Sawyer if he had seen April and Ethan Allen. Mr. Sawyer was sitting on an old wicker chair on his front porch with the newspaper in front of him. I think he was asleep and the sound of my bike on the gravel woke him up. He rattled the pages of his newspaper as if he were reading it. But he didn't have any news of the missing pair either.

After the Sawyer house, the road becomes paved and leads into the highway. I rode my bike south, in the direction of our town. The traffic was getting heavy, as it always does at that time of day: people driving home from work, people going home to cook supper. I hoped that April and Ethan Allen knew to keep close to the side. Did April know you're supposed to walk facing traffic? Maybe she had gone to buy an ice-cream cone, I thought. Then I remembered that April never had any real money in her pocket. I stopped at the ice-cream stand anyhow and looked around. My Little League baseball team plays every Thursday evening. After the game we always come here, and the parents who've watched us play treat us to cones. With all the players and their parents, there are a lot of cars and people standing around waiting their turn. Now there was just one car, with a Florida license plate. The Florida couple was debating: Did they want vanilla or chocolate, ice cream or frozen yogurt?

"Did you see a little girl and a llama as you were driving by?" I asked them anxiously.

"A llama?" asked the woman. "Here in Vermont?"

So I knew right away that they hadn't seen her.

I pedaled on down the road and stopped at the Grand Union. April and Ethan Allen weren't in the parking lot, and since there is a notice outside that says No Dogs Allowed, I knew for sure that they wouldn't let a llama inside either. Then I pedaled over to the post office. There was no sign of April or Ethan Allen there. They weren't at the barbershop or the gas station.

A police car with a flashing light and blaring siren passed me as I cycled down the road. It was headed north, toward my house. A shudder went through me. Maybe April and Ethan Allen were in big trouble. Maybe they'd been hit by a car.

I felt hot and tired, so I got off my bike and sat on the overgrown lawn in front of the Mountain View

Inn. The inn is closed now, and there is a big For Sale sign outside it.

I was so sweaty that my plastic lanyard with the whistle on the end was sticking to my neck. I rubbed my hand under it, and suddenly I got an idea. I don't know why I hadn't thought of it before. I put the whistle in my mouth and gave a loud blast. I stopped for a breath and then I blew it again and again.

When I finally stopped, I listened carefully. I heard a truck changing gears along the road. There was also a mosquito buzzing near my ear. But those weren't the sounds I was listening for. I was just about to blow the whistle again when I heard a high-pitched hum. Only one thing makes a noise like that. I turned around to see where the sound was coming from. It took a moment before I spotted them. But there was Ethan Allen, and there, holding on to his long hair, was April. They were coming right toward me. It was the happiest moment of my life!

"Hi, Adam," April called out to me. She said it as if we were in our yard at home and not just off the highway, over a mile away.

"Where have you been?" I asked her. "Mom is looking all over for you. And so are the police."

"The police?" April's eyes grew wide. "Will they put me in jail? I didn't do anything bad."

"No, silly. They are looking for you because you were lost."

"I wasn't lost at all," said April. "E-N-L-N was walking and I was walking with him. I saw him break the fence. Then he started going down the road and I thought I better go with him because he doesn't know the way. So we just kept walking and walking. I wasn't lost and neither was E-N-L-N because I told him where we were."

"Well, we better hurry home and tell Mom where you are too," I said.

"Okay," said April. "Could you pick me up and put me on E-N-L-N's back? I'm awfully tired."

I helped April up on the llama's back.

"Hold tight," I told her.

She clutched Ethan Allen by the long hair on his back, and I turned him around toward our house. It wasn't easy walking uphill, pushing my bike with one hand and holding on to the llama with the other. I kept an eye on April because now that I had found her, I didn't want her falling off and getting hurt.

"Guess what," said April, beaming down at me from her perch on Ethan Allen's back. "I didn't suck my thumb the whole time. I couldn't because I was so busy holding on to E-N-L-N and watching where I was going."

"Well, that's good," I said. "But next time, if he goes out of the yard, you better call Mom to catch him. The two of you could have gotten hit by a car or something."

Just then a car coming toward us pulled to a halt. It had a Florida license plate. The window rolled down and a voice called out, "Well, you found him. And it really is a llama."

"And my sister too," I added.

We made it the rest of the way home. The woods behind our house were filled with policemen with walkie-talkies. It was pretty exciting to see so much action on our property. I'd have a lot to tell my friends when I saw them the next day.

My mom and dad—he'd come home from his store—were very relieved to see April. Dad said he was very proud of me for finding them. I explained to him about blowing on my whistle. I always said it was the best trick that I had taught Ethan Allen.

6
The Braided Rug

❏ ❏ ❏ ❏ ❏ ❏ ❏ ❏ ❏ ❏

Blueberry season was over, and zucchini season had begun. It was also fishing season. At least once a week, I went either with my dad or Justin's or Larry's father. Each father had his favorite fishing spot, and each filled his boat with boys, bait, and rods and off we'd go. There is something very special about sitting in a boat as the sun goes down. All is still except for the ripple of the water and the little splash as we cast our lines into the lake.

Justin, Larry, and I had made a bet about who would catch the most fish before the summer was out. The winner would be treated to a hot fudge sundae by the two other guys. By the end of July, we were pretty close. One evening Justin was in the lead; on another, Larry caught three trout and he edged ahead. Some evenings none of us caught anything. But it didn't really matter. Sitting in a boat and fishing is part of summer. And not catching anything is part of summer also.

That's the way my mother's business was going too. Some weeks there were no bites on her line at all; others, she'd have two or three groups of people going out for llama treks. One week, when she had gone out three different times, I watched as she added up the money she had received from her customers.

"Are you making a lot of money?" I asked hopefully.

"We're getting there," she said. "Don't think I've forgotten your bike."

I grinned. It looked as if soon I'd have both a mountain bike and the only llama in town after all. Not bad, I thought.

The next evening, Dad took Justin, Larry, and me fishing. It was a good night for me. I caught two trout, big enough so I didn't have to throw them back. Justin caught a little one that was undersized, and Larry didn't get anything that evening at all.

On the way home, I sat in the back of the pickup truck with Justin and Larry. For some reason we started singing as we rode along. We'd never done it before, but in the dark, as we bumped over the ruts in the dirt road, it just seemed like the right thing to do. I don't know who started it, but soon we were all singing, "Old MacDonald had a farm...." We'd mooed and crowed and barked by the time we reached Justin's house.

"I think I can taste that sundae already," I said, licking my lips and grinning as we dropped him off. Even in the dark you could see the shining scales of my two fish as I held them up.

Larry and I continued singing. I sang out, "And on that farm he had a llama, E-I-E-I-O." Then I tried to imitate Ethan Allen with one of his famous hums here and hums there, everywhere a hum, hum, when the pickup stopped in front of Larry's house.

"Don't be so sure of that ice cream," teased Larry when he got out of the truck. "My father said he'd take us to Somerset Reservoir next week. I always have good luck there."

I jumped out of the back of the truck and went to sit next to my father. He slowed the truck as we passed someone riding a bike along the side of the road.

"You need more reflectors," my father shouted to the rider. "Better still, you shouldn't ride on a dark road at night."

"When I get my new bike, I'll be careful about riding in the dark," I promised him. I was feeling pretty good, what with my two fish in the back of the truck and the thought of a new bike before the summer was over.

That's when Dad said something that I wasn't expecting.

"Listen, Adam," he said. "I know how much you've been counting on a new bike. But there are a lot of other things around the house that we need too. Things that are more important than a bike."

"What's more important than a new bike for me?" I demanded. My good mood was disappearing fast.

"You know how your mother is always complaining about what a pain it is to defrost the refrigerator? Well, that's because it's about thirty years old. It came with the house when we bought it. It works all right, but she really deserves a modern, self-defrosting one. They aren't cheap. So what do you say about holding off with the bike?"

I could feel my face getting hot, and I didn't know what to say. In a way, it was a compliment that my dad was talking to me man-to-man, but that didn't mean I didn't want a new bike. Mom had promised me I'd get one when her business picked up. Now the business was going fine and Dad was trying to talk me out of the bike. It didn't seem fair.

"The longer you wait, the longer your legs will be," he pointed out. "Then you can get an adult-sized bike. It makes more sense to do that than to get a smaller bike that you'll outgrow in a year or two."

What he said would have made sense if I didn't

have to ride the old bike every day. I couldn't wait a couple of years for a new bike. I just couldn't.

That's when I realized once and for all that I would have to get a bike on my own, without taking any money from my parents. I thought of ways I could make money. I could pick wild blackberries and sell them for a couple of bucks a quart. But it would take thousands and thousands of berries before I would earn enough money. There had to be a better way.

I began reading and rereading my mother's magazines. There must be something that I could trade away.

Will swap fine English antique pitcher and bowl for small crazy quilt in good condition.

Will swap two weeks in my three-bedroom/two-bath chalet in Vermont for two weeks in your home in London, England.

Will swap large braided rug for microwave oven.

I stopped when I read that last ad. It seemed to me that we had one of those old braided rugs in our attic. I threw down the magazine and charged up the stairs. I pulled down the trapdoor that leads to our unfinished attic. I didn't want to waste a second. The attic was hot and musty-smelling. It was filled with all sorts of stuff. There were boxes labeled *baby clothes*. The carriage Mom had used first with me and then with April was there. There was a pile of my mom's old college books and stacks of old *National Geographic* magazines.

I pushed the magazines aside, and, sure enough, there was the old braided rug I'd noticed the last time I was hunting for something in the attic.

I remembered my mother saying that the rug had been there when they bought the house. My parents didn't particularly want it, but for some lucky reason, they had never gotten around to throwing it out. There it had been all these years, collecting dust and probably keeping some mice warm during the winter too.

It was rolled up, so I couldn't inspect it very well. I didn't have any idea about what sort of condition it was in. But one thing I knew as soon as I tried to lift it: It was big. My heart began beating fast. I was pretty certain that my parents would let me have the rug. Of course, I didn't want to trade it for a microwave oven. We already had one of those. But if one person wanted a braided rug, there were certain to be others who did too. I could sell our rug and get money for my bike!

"Sure you can have it," my mother said.

"I'll help you take it down," my father offered.

So after supper, the two of us went up to the attic. We each took an end and came down the stairs carrying the rolled-up rug. Along the way, my father sneezed three times from the dust. I sneezed twice. We took it outside and hung it over the porch rail so we could see it better. I attempted to beat out some of the dust.

That old braided rug must have been sitting up in our attic for years and years. My parents have owned our house for ten years, but the house is about eighty years old; the rug may be that old too.

Dad, of course, looked at it with a professional eye. After all, his work is selling rugs and carpets. But none of his customers want old things. They all want modern nylon carpets with colors that have fancy names like *rhubarb* and *magnolia*.

"This is the real McCoy," my father said. "Look." He pointed to the way the strips of fabric were braided together. "Nowadays, if you go out to buy a braided rug, you'll notice that the strips are just twisted together by machine to look as if they are braided. Too bad it hasn't been kept in better shape," he said, showing me where the original stitching was coming out and the strips of braid were coming apart.

"Can it be fixed?" I asked.

"I'll help you," he offered. "But what are you

going to do with it then? Do you want it for your bedroom?"

"No. I want to see if I can sell it to one of the dealers at the flea market."

"A second generation of Fines is entering the floor-covering business," he laughed.

He went inside and came back with a thick needle and some heavy thread. Since my mother is so bad about sewing buttons and things, it really was a kind of miracle that he could find that stuff. It was still light out, so he threaded the needle and began to sew one of the strips of rug that had separated from the rest.

"Look," he said, showing me. "These old braided rugs were made up of all sorts of old clothing."

I could see that there was a bit of flowered material that had been used. Maybe it had been a dress that had belonged to the woman who lived in this house eighty years ago. There was also a lot of navy blue cloth. Maybe those were her husband's pants. It was as if a whole history was pulled together and stitched into this rug.

Ethan Allen stopped eating his supper of grass and walked over to investigate. He sniffed at the braided rug and then turned back to the grass. What did he care about rugs and history?

By the time it had gotten too dark to see on the porch, my father had mended the rug in several places. "That's enough for tonight," he said. "Besides, don't you want to watch the Red Sox game?"

So we folded up the rug and brought it inside. My mom made a big batch of popcorn, and we all sat together watching the baseball game on TV. Even April sat with us until she fell asleep.

After that, each evening Dad would work a little on the braided rug. He even showed me how to do it, so that I was able to sew some of it too. I probably could have taken it to the flea market that weekend, but I decided to wait until it was completely fixed up. On Saturday, I went empty-handed to the flea market and just walked about, looking for that bike that was never going to be there. Justin was with me. We looked at everything, the way we always do. You never know what you're going to see. Then I grabbed his arm and pulled him over to the guy who sells quilts and rugs. Justin knew my plan, and now he watched as I looked around at the stuff for sale.

"How much is that crazy quilt?" I asked the man, just to make conversation.

"Two hundred dollars," he said.

I was stunned.

Justin let out a whistle of surprise. Most things at the flea market sell for loads less. Occasionally, someone will have a few pieces of heavy furniture that they've refinished and are selling for a hundred or two hundred dollars. But I never dreamed that a quilt would cost so much. I was glad I wasn't trying to raise enough money for a crazy quilt.

"Each of these stitches was done by hand," the dealer said, taking the quilt and opening it up.

I looked at the quilt. Instead of having a regular pattern, it was made up of all odd-sized pieces and fabrics. Some were of soft velvet and others were shiny satin. They were attached together in a way so the stitches would show. The stitches were in black or red thread and looked sort of like chicken tracks around each piece. Usually stitching isn't supposed to show, but in a crazy quilt, the stitches are part of the design. I've learned a lot about things like that from hanging about the flea market.

"What about that braided rug?" I asked, nodding toward one that was rolled up and lying on the ground. "How much does that cost?"

"Seventy-five," he said. "How come a kid like you is interested in all these household articles? Are you planning to get married or something?"

Even though I knew he was joking, I could feel my ears turning red and hot. Justin started laughing, which made it worse. "My mom is interested in things like this," I mumbled. "Can I see the rug?"

Since there was no one else around to inspect his stuff, the guy shrugged his shoulders. "Why not?" he said.

He unrolled the braided rug and right away I felt

great. It was much smaller than the one from our attic. Also, it had boring colors: all brown and tan with a little green. Mine was much more lively, with blues and reds and the cloth with the flowers on it. I bent down and examined it more closely. The strips of fabric had just been twisted together. It wasn't a *real* braided rug at all.

"Oh, isn't that beautiful," a woman's voice said behind me. If she was interested in buying, she had just made a fatal error. She would never be able to bargain down the price now.

"How much is that old rug?" asked the man with her. I guess he was her husband.

"Eighty-five dollars," said the dealer, without missing a beat.

I tried to catch his eye, but he made a point of looking away from me. So I looked at Justin instead. Neither of us said a word.

"Harold. It would look perfect in our family room," said the woman. "The colors go with the sofa and the wood paneling."

"Is eighty-five the best price you can give?" Harold asked the dealer.

"Yeah. I won't even make any profit on it. But it takes up a lot of room, so I'm willing to part with it for that. It's antique, you know."

"Looks like it's falling apart," said Harold.

"Anyone could fix it up easily with a needle and

thread and a spare hour," said the dealer.

"I could mend it," whispered Harold's wife. It wasn't much of a whisper. Justin and I could hear her and so could the dealer.

"I don't know," said Harold. "Maybe we should think about it," he said to his wife.

"Sure," said the dealer. "But I got to warn you, there was another couple here just a few minutes ago. They're thinking about it too. So it might not be here when you get back."

"Oh, Harold," the woman moaned.

Harold stuck his hand in his pocket and pulled out his wallet. "How about eighty?" he asked as he took four twenty-dollar bills and showed them to the dealer.

The dealer scratched his head and appeared to be thinking. "All right," he said reluctantly. "Eighty in the hand is worth eighty-five in the bush, as they say."

Harold paid the money, and the dealer rolled up the rug and tied it with a piece of rope.

"Enjoy it," said the dealer as the couple went off smiling. "You got yourselves a real good bargain there. I've seen those same rugs for a hundred in a couple of fancy antique shops."

When they were gone, the dealer turned to me finally and winked. "Well," he said. "Everyone's happy. Harold saved five dollars, so he's happy. His wife got the rug she wanted, so she's happy. And I just unloaded a big piece of merchandise for more than I thought I'd get, so I'm happy."

I nodded my head in agreement. I was feeling pretty happy myself.

"If that old torn brown-and-tan rug sold for eighty dollars, then the one I have at home is worth close to two hundred," I said to Justin as soon as we walked off. "That mountain bike is as good as mine!" I felt like jumping, not walking. I could already imagine myself riding down the road on the new bike.

"Hey, don't be so sure," warned Justin. "Maybe he won't want to buy it from you. Did you ever think of that?"

"No," I said. But suddenly I felt a little less sure of myself. "Why wouldn't he buy it? It's better than the one he just sold."

"You'll have to wait and see," said Justin. "Things don't always work out just the way you want them to."

He didn't have to tell me. I already knew that.

7
The Big Swap

❑ ❑ ❑ ❑ ❑ ❑ ❑ ❑ ❑ ❑

By Wednesday of the following week, the braided rug was completely mended. At my mother's suggestion, I left it out in the sun for a full day so that some of the musty smell would disappear. It was rolled up and ready for Saturday, when I planned to take it to the dealer at the flea market. I was sure that the size and quality of that rug, combined with my bargaining skills, would enable me to work out a good deal. Furthermore, having seen and heard the dealer in action, we both knew he would be able to unload the rug to a customer at a profit.

I'm sure the reason I played so well in Little League on Thursday evening, hitting my first home run of the season, was that I was feeling so great. When one thing goes well, it gives you the energy and confidence to make other things work out well too.

On Friday morning I heard the weekend weather

forecast. I couldn't believe it when they said that rainstorms were expected for both Saturday and Sunday. The flea market is held outdoors, and although it's supposed to be open every weekend all summer, almost no one shows up in the rain. You can't blame them. The dealers don't want to get their stuff wet, and the customers don't want to get themselves wet.

Maybe the weatherman would be wrong. On Friday morning the sun was shining and the day looked glorious. But by evening, the wind was blowing all the leaves in our trees, and that's a real sign that the weather is about to change. Sure enough, I woke on Saturday morning to a big downpour. Maybe it would stop for Sunday, I thought. But really that wouldn't be good enough. Many of the dealers who exhibit at the flea market come a great distance. They sleep in the backs of their pickup trucks or in campers. Some stay at one of the local motels. It's not worth their while to make the trip for only a one-day sale. Now I'd have to wait till the next weekend. And suppose it rained then too?

It just didn't seem fair.

My mother had to cancel a llama trek that she had scheduled. "Six customers, down the drain," she said unhappily.

With all that rain, "down the drain" was exactly the right expression. Justin was spending the weekend at our house while his parents went out of town. Any other time I would have been very glad to have him staying over, especially if the weather was bad and I was stuck inside the house. But now I felt so let down after waiting all week for Saturday that nothing we could do was able to distract me. My disappointment made me restless.

"We could play cards," suggested Justin.

"Naw. That's boring," I complained.

"You want to play with your trains?" he asked. We used to play with an old train set that had belonged to my father when he was a kid, but today that seemed dull too.

"Too bad we can't go outside and groom Ethan Allen," said Justin.

The rain was coming down so hard that the llama was hiding in the stable. On wet days, his hair was extra-hard to comb. I thought about Ethan Allen alone in the stable. It must be boring for him today too. Eating grass and going on hiking trips was fine part of the time, but there must be other times when he felt lonely for another of his own species. Too bad there wasn't another llama in the stable, keeping him company.

Lunch was the food my mother had fixed for her trekkers: curried chicken salad, pasta salad, oatmeal bread, and homemade applesauce made from the apples that had fallen off the two old apple trees at the end of our property. There were whole-wheat brownies for dessert.

April took a nap after lunch. My mother said she thought it was a good idea, so she went to take a nap too. My father was off doing a big job, carpeting a living room–dining room for some summer people who had just bought a house in the area. Molly Stark was sleeping in a corner of the living room sofa. Justin and I were the only ones awake inside the house.

I sat at the opposite end of the sofa from Molly Stark and picked up the latest issue of my mother's *New England* magazine. It had just come that morning in the mail. I wondered what people were trading this month. Justin had been flipping the TV dial, but he turned off the set in disgust. There was nothing good on at that hour. He came over, sat down next to me, and looked over my shoulder as I read:

Will swap new hand-embroidered 52" x 70" tablecloth for set of four cast-iron frying pans.

Will swap down-draft wood-burning stove for aluminum canoe.

Will swap male llama for crazy quilt in excellent condition.

The tiny letters on the page jumped out at me.

"Look at that!" I shouted to Justin. I pointed to the line I had just read. "Someone has a llama to swap." At that moment, I suddenly knew that I had to try and get that llama. Getting a second llama seemed much more important to me than getting a new bike.

"Instead of selling my braided rug to the dealer at the flea market, I could make a swap with him. I could trade my braided rug for the crazy quilt he has. Then I could swap the crazy quilt with the person who has the llama." It was a fantastic plan.

"By the time you trade the rug, the llama will be gone," said Justin. "It won't work. Besides, I thought you wanted to sell it so you could buy yourself a bike."

I shrugged my shoulders. "Anyone can have a bike," I pointed out. "My mother could use a second llama for her business. And Ethan Allen needs a llama for a friend. If he had a companion llama, he wouldn't go walking off down the road." The more I talked, the more I convinced myself how important it was to get another llama. "Soon school will be open, and neither April or I will be around to talk to Ethan Allen. And when the weather gets cool, the tourists won't want to go on llama treks. What's going to happen to Ethan Allen during the winter? We'll be skiing or snowmobiling or ice-skating. But for Ethan Allen, it's sure going to be a long lonely time."

Justin began to see my point. "You won't be able to ride a bike in the snow," he said.

"Right." I nodded. I wished we could go to the flea market right that moment. Suppose the dealer had sold the crazy quilt during the week. I bit two nails as I thought about the complications that might get in the way of my plan. Then I calmed down and read the instructions about how to answer the ads in the magazine. After each ad there was a code number. You had to write to the magazine, giving the code number of the ad you were responding to. You also had to send a stamped envelope for forwarding. It was funny how the identities and the addresses of the people who wanted to do the swapping were kept secret. I'd never noticed that before.

At least writing a letter was something I could do on a rainy day. I ran and got a piece of paper, and Justin and I sat at the kitchen table while I wrote.

"Tell them that you already have a llama," suggested Justin. "That way they'll see that you know all about taking care of one."

It seemed like a good idea, so I included that in my letter. I said I had a lovely crazy quilt to trade. I didn't say that I didn't actually own the quilt yet. I figured by the time #2JZ4 got my letter and wrote back to me, I'd have the crazy quilt in hand.

Once I finished writing the letter, addressing the envelope, and finding two stamps in my mother's desk, I couldn't wait to mail it. I wanted the person who had the llama to get my letter first. Maybe there were loads of people with crazy quilts who were dying to get llamas. If my letter got there first, I'd have a better chance.

Justin wanted to come along, so we put on our rain slickers. I stuck the letter in my pocket and got my bike out of the shed. Ethan Allen was in there smelling like a wet sweater, even though he was indoors. I guess it was all the humidity in the air that made him get that way.

"Ethan Allen," I said. "There may be a big surprise for you very soon."

Then I remembered that I didn't even have the crazy quilt that I had offered to trade away. And perhaps nothing would come of this big plan of mine after all.

"Listen, Ethan Allen. Forget what I said. Think of something else, okay? How are those leaves you're eating? Are they good? Would you like a few cold rolled oats?"

I poured some of the oats into the pail and offered them to the llama.

He gave one of his funny whines and stuck his head inside the pail. If we got a second llama, we'd have to get a second pail so they could both have treats at the same time.

I got on my bike and Justin climbed on behind

me, since his bike was over at his house. It was hard pedaling, what with the muddy road and Justin's weight. But at two-thirty there we were, dripping wet in front of the post office. I'd forgotten that on a Saturday afternoon, the post office is closed. But I pulled the letter out of my pocket and dropped it in the mailbox out front. I was glad to see that the mail would be picked up at 4:45 P.M. That should mean that my letter would get to the magazine by Monday. If they addressed and sent off my envelope to the llama owner the same day, by Wednesday he or she would get my letter. I had included my phone number in the letter. I couldn't bear to wait longer than Wednesday to know if the llama was still available.

"Don't say anything to anyone about this," I said to Justin. "Let's keep it a surprise."

"Who do you think will be the most surprised if this swap comes off?" asked Justin. "Your mother or Ethan Allen?"

"I don't know," I said. "Maybe it will be me."

The next days crawled by. Sometimes I'd forget for a little while when I was busy doing something like racing some of the guys to the raft in the middle of the lake. Then I only thought about swimming. But once I reached the raft (I came in second, ahead of Greg Cox but after Doug Henderson) and I was catching my breath, I remembered again.

80 ❑

On Wednesday I didn't want to go anywhere. I wanted to stay home and wait for the phone call. That was a pretty stupid thing to do because no one phoned me, and it was a terribly long, boring, tense day. Since they didn't call on Wednesday, I was sure they'd call on Thursday. Wrong.

"How come you don't want to go off to the lake?" my mother asked as she was packing up for a llama trek. "Do you feel okay?"

"Oh, I've got things to do around here," I lied.

I still hadn't told her about the plan. I was bursting to tell her, but I decided not to just yet. After I had made the arrangements for the exchange, there would be time enough. If the whole deal fell through, she'd be disappointed, just the way I was about not getting my bike. The funny thing is that all that week while I was waiting for the phone call, I never thought that if the deal didn't work out, I'd at least be able to get the money for the bike. The bike no longer seemed to matter. I'd be getting one eventually. But a llama...

No one phoned on Thursday. Maybe my letter had gotten lost in the mail. Maybe they had changed their mind about the trade. We wouldn't want to trade Ethan Allen. Maybe they'd already traded their llama for someone else's crazy quilt. There were so many possibilities I thought I'd go crazy, like the quilt, myself.

Friday morning while I was eating breakfast, the telephone rang. My mother's friend Eileen often calls in the morning, so I just assumed that's who it was. But my mother handed me the phone. "It's for you," she said, raising her eyebrows in surprise. "I don't recognize the voice," she whispered.

I swallowed the piece of toast in my mouth. This was it, I realized. This must be it, the call I had been waiting for.

"Hello," I said. My voice sounded strange to me. I guess it was because there was still a little toast clinging to the inside of my mouth.

"Is this Adam Fine?" asked a man's voice on the other end.

"Yes it is."

"Fine," said the voice. Then he laughed. I laughed too. He laughed because he thought he'd made a joke. I laughed with relief that he'd finally called.

"My name is George Lindsey. I live in Peru, Vermont. That's not too far from Wilmington, maybe an hour's drive. After our last dog died, my wife and I thought having a llama would be a great pet. A great pet and a good joke. After all, llamas come from Peru. Peru, South America, Peru, Vermont. Get it?" he asked.

"Yeah," I said. I laughed again. He was as crazy as the quilt too, I thought.

"Well. We've had Macintosh for two years. He's a wonderful animal. We just love him. But now we've sold our house. We're moving to Florida. It's not the right climate for a llama. But we don't want Macintosh to go to just any old home. So my wife and I would like to meet you. And check out the crazy quilt at the same time. She's always admired them in antique shops, but we never wanted to spend the money on one. This seemed like the perfect swap. What do you say?"

"Macintosh. That's a computer," I said. It was a pretty stupid thing to say, but it just popped out of my mouth.

"Macintosh is an apple. It was an apple long before anyone ever heard of computers. And my family is from Scotland originally," the man explained. "Macintosh is a good Scottish name."

"Oh, yeah," I agreed. I imagined a whole herd of llamas named Winesap, Delicious, and Granny Smith.

"So what do you say, Adam? Would you like to come today?" asked the man.

"I can't come today," I said quickly. For one thing, I didn't have the crazy quilt yet. For another, I would have to arrange for my father to drive me to Peru in his pickup truck. That way we could bring the llama back home with us. We'd bring Macintosh home with us if everything worked out, that is.

"How about Sunday?" I asked. I needed time to go to the flea market, and, remembering that my father often had to work on Saturdays, I thought it would be safer to plan for the day after.

Mr. Lindsey gave me directions to his home. It didn't sound very hard. "Okay," I said finally. "I'll see you then."

After I hung up, I realized I should have gotten his phone number. Suppose when Sunday came I didn't have a crazy quilt to swap for his llama?

8

A Sunday Surprise

❏ ❏ ❏ ❏ ❏ ❏ ❏ ❏ ❏ ❏

That August weekend turned out to be full of events for my family. They began Saturday morning when Molly Stark caught her first mouse. Actually, she might have caught the mouse on Friday night, but my mom discovered the corpse when she went into the kitchen Saturday morning. Luckily, April was still sleeping, so there were no explanations needed. I came into the kitchen just after my mother had picked up the mouse with a paper towel and was putting it into the garbage pail.

"Poor thing," she sighed.

"Maybe the word will go out in the mouse world that this is a good house to keep away from," I said, by way of consolation.

Molly Stark rubbed herself against my bare leg. I bent down to pet her and thought about how smart she was. We got her to help us get rid of mice, and without our ever explaining the job to her, she had done it. Maybe her mother had meowed the message to her when she was a tiny kitten.

So that was how the weekend began. I was up early because I was eager to get to the flea market with the braided rug. My mom still didn't know what was going on. She was very curious about the phone conversation I'd had the morning before. But she didn't bother me about it like some mothers would. I guess she figured that I'd tell her when I was ready. However, I had to tell Dad the whole story. Without his help, there was no way I could move the heavy braided rug from our house to the flea market. And without his help, there was no way I could get to Peru on Sunday, either.

I was nervous about whether the crazy quilt would still be for sale. I had told Mr. Lindsey that I had a quilt to swap with him. It would be terrible to come this close to a deal and not to have one after all. It would make me out to be a liar, and it would probably be the end of any kind of arrangement.

Ethan Allen watched as my father and I loaded the braided rug into the pickup truck. "Won't he be surprised if my plan works out?" I asked my father.

"He sure will. And so will your mother," my father said. "Are you certain this is what you want to do with the rug? You can probably get enough money to buy that bike you've been begging for."

"I know," I said. "But, like you said, if I wait a couple of years, my legs will be longer and I can get an adult-sized bike."

"It's nice to know you listen to me," said my dad, squeezing my shoulder.

We were good and early at the flea market, which was great. After we parked the pickup, I directed my father toward the spot where the quilt and rug dealer usually set up. Suppose he didn't come this weekend? I asked myself. It was another of the possibilities that I had been worrying about.

But there he was, sitting in his collapsible lawn chair and drinking coffee from a paper cup. I let out a sigh of relief.

"What have you got there?" he asked when we stopped in front of him.

My dad and I put the braided rug down on the ground. "I'm interested in making a trade with you," I said.

"What kind of a trade?" he asked.

"Do you still have that old crazy quilt I saw here a couple of weeks ago?"

"Nope. I got lucky and I sold it," he said.

"You mean it's gone?" I asked incredulously. "I wanted to make a trade with you." At that moment I thought I was going to start crying like April does when she's had a disappointment.

"Yep. It was a beauty and in perfect condition. That's quite unusual. Often those old quilts are frayed with age," he said.

I stood there limp and miserable. All my plans had revolved around this man's crazy quilt. And it was gone, just like Justin had warned me could happen.

"What do you want for that rug?" the man asked me.

I sighed. I didn't even care about selling the rug now. But my dad gave me a poke. "What do you think your rug is worth, Adam?" he asked me.

"Two hundred and fifty dollars," I said. My voice came out in a hoarse whisper.

"Speak up," said the man. "I can't hear you."

"Two hundred and fifty dollars," I said a bit louder.

My father didn't say a word. He just stood there watching me as I stooped to untie the rope that held the rug rolled up.

"There's no braided rug that valuable," said the dealer, draining the last of his coffee. Still, he bent over to see what the rug looked like.

"It's easily twice the size of the one you sold a couple of weeks ago," I pointed out to him. Maybe if I sold the rug, I could bring the money to the Lindseys and convince them to buy their own quilt with it.

"This is in perfect condition," I added. "There's

not a single hole in it. And look at the colors. And most important, this is real braid, not some fabrics machine-twisted to look like braid. It's beautiful!" I'd said it all, and then I had to stop and catch my breath.

The dealer burst out laughing. "Kid. Do you want to come and work for me? You're great at this. Where did you learn it all?"

I turned red. I didn't know if he meant it or if he was just teasing me. "I learned it all from you," I said. "I come here almost every week, and I've heard you talking to the customers. I've seen a few things too."

"So you do. So you have," said the dealer. He got down on his hands and knees and examined the braided rug more closely. While he was looking at it, I looked at my father. He gave me the thumbs-up signal. He knew and I knew that I had a deal going.

"Tell you what," said the man. "I'll buy your rug for fifty bucks. That's a lot of money for a kid your age."

"No way," I said, standing firm. "I'll go sell this rug to someone else for three hundred dollars and come back and show you the money."

The dealer let out a whistle. "You'll never get three hundred dollars for a braided rug. Two hundred if you're really lucky. But never three."

"Well, if I can get two hundred, then you can get three," I said. "I'll give it to you for two." That's the way those dealers talk. *Give*, they always say. *I'll give it to you*, when they mean *sell*.

I held my breath and waited.

"Oh, what an exquisite braided rug," a woman's voice exclaimed.

I couldn't help myself. Even though I was still feeling disappointed about the crazy quilt, I found myself grinning. I didn't know that woman from Adam (and I was Adam!), but she had just played into my hands.

"How much is it?" the woman asked the dealer.

"Just a minute," he said to her. "You take a look at the quality of this rug while I conclude a little business with this young man here."

"Ed," he called to a guy at the next booth. "Keep an eye on my stuff for me for a minute, will ya?"

Ed nodded.

"Okay," said the dealer, turning to me. "Just keep calm. I'll be back in a minute." And then he rushed off.

"Where do you think he went?" I asked my father.

"To the john?" my father suggested, shrugging his shoulders. Then he put his arm around me. "Listen, Adam," he said. "If the trade for the llama doesn't work out, at least now you'll be able to buy yourself a pretty good bike."

90 ❏

"I know," I said. It was so strange. A week ago I would never have thought that the chance to get money to buy myself a new bike would mean so little to me.

Suddenly the rug dealer was back, and he was holding a paper bag. "Okay," he said. "How's this for a trade?"

I opened the bag and let out a gasp. There was a crazy quilt every bit as pretty as the one he had displayed two weeks before. In fact, I thought it was a little bigger.

"Where did this come from?" I asked. It seemed like some sort of magic to me.

"Another dealer showed it to me this morning when we were all unpacking our stuff. So, is it a trade?" he asked.

"Yes, sir!" I said, holding tight to the quilt.

I wanted to hang around in the worst way so I could see how much money he got for the braided rug. But my father gave me a little push. "Come on," he said softly. "You got what you wanted."

He dropped me off at the house on the way to his store. He had a job installing a tile floor in someone's kitchen and would be busy all morning. I let him hold on to the crazy quilt for me because there was no way I could get it into the house without my mom seeing it. And having gone this far with the surprise, I was determined to go all the way. She'd find out about everything tomorrow, after the rest of the swap was completed.

After breakfast on Sunday, my father and I were ready to take a ride together. "We'll be back in a little while," he called to my mother.

"I want to go too," begged April.

Dad looked at me. "Okay," I agreed. So the three of us got into the cab of the pickup and started driving north.

"Where are we going?" asked April.

"Peru," I told her.

"Where's that?" she wanted to know.

"It's nearby," Dad said.

"It's far away too," I said. "It depends which Peru you mean."

"Why are we going there?" April demanded.

"We're getting a surprise for Mom," I said.

"A surprise!" April looked all excited. "What is it?"

"You'll see. Very soon," I promised.

"Daddy. Will you tell me what it is?" April asked him.

"Nope. Just be patient. It's a very good surprise. Worth waiting for." He took his eyes from the road and looked over at me and winked. Then he said, "April. You have a pretty good fellow for a brother. Did you know that?"

"Yes," said April, nodding her head seriously.

I felt my face getting red, so I looked down and opened the paper bag on my lap that contained the crazy quilt. It was too crowded in the front seat of the pickup to spread it out. But I admired even the little that I could see. All the pieces that made it up had been cut out by hand. I wondered just who it was who had sewn it all together and when they had done it. Wouldn't whoever made it have been amazed if they knew that this quilt was going to be exchanged for a llama!

I started worrying about whether Mr. and Mrs. Lindsey—who owned the llama—would be satisfied with the crazy quilt I was bringing. Maybe they had seen other quilts that they liked even better. Maybe they would say that they didn't want to make a swap after all. That would be an awful surprise.

Peru, Vermont, looks exactly like my town. It's just the name that sounds foreign. Mr. and Mrs. Lindsey's house was on a dirt road, and I knew it was the right place because they had a little yellow sign with a picture of a llama. It was like those road signs you see warning you of a deer crossing. This was a llama-crossing sign.

I looked about for Macintosh. And there he was. But to my surprise, unlike Ethan Allen, Macintosh had dark brown hair.

April jumped down from the pickup truck and

went to hug the brown llama. "Look," she called with excitement. "I didn't know llamas came in other colors. Is this the surprise?"

I nodded my head, hoping I was right. We wouldn't know until the Lindseys made it final.

Mr. and Mrs. Lindsey came out of their house, and we all introduced ourselves. I was holding on to the bag with the crazy quilt, and I handed it to Mrs. Lindsey. "I hope it's okay," I said.

Mrs. Lindsey sat down on a wooden lawn chair and spread the quilt out on her lap. "It's lovely," she said, touching the pieces gently. "It makes you wonder about who it was that made this beautiful cover."

"I was thinking the same thing," I said, smiling.

My father spoke with Mr. Lindsey and told him that our llama needed a friend.

"That's absolutely so," agreed Mr. Lindsey. "Llamas are very sociable animals. They need companions. Just like kids." He turned and winked at April and me. "We always thought we might get another llama to keep Macintosh company. But we never did."

Mr. Lindsey smiled at April, who was still petting the brown llama. "So I'm really glad Macintosh is going to people who have another llama. And it's great that there are young people as well. Macintosh loves children."

"Mr. Lindsey," I said. "I've got a question."

"Yes?" asked the man.

"How come you decided to swap your llama to us? You could get a lot of money if you sold him. You'd have enough to buy yourself a crazy quilt and more left over."

"You're absolutely right," agreed Mr. Lindsey. "But, you know, Macintosh is like a member of our family. And my wife and I agreed that we just couldn't sell him for money. You don't sell family. So instead, we thought about trying one of these exchange things that we've been reading about for years in the magazine. And now we see that it works. Macintosh is going to a good home, which makes us feel better about parting with him. And the crazy quilt is like a bonus for my wife. I think if we'd known about you folks, we just would have handed Mac over and not asked for anything in exchange."

So the trade was made, just as I planned it. We got Macintosh up on the ramp and into the truck. April was grinning from ear to ear. She loved the new member of our family, and she loved the fact that it was all a big surprise for our mother.

Just before we got into the truck, I thought of something. "Mr. Lindsey," I asked. "Would it be okay if we gave Macintosh a new name?"

"What's wrong with Macintosh?" asked Mr. Lindsey.

"It's a great name for an apple or a computer," I

said. "But my mom has this thing about Vermont llamas having Vermont names. We already have Ethan Allen living with us. So I think this llama should be called Ira. That was the name of Ethan Allen's brother," I reminded him.

"So it was," said Mr. Lindsey. "The house where he used to live is only about ten miles from here."

"Is it all right?" I asked him again.

"If Macintosh doesn't mind, then neither do I," said Mr. Lindsey.

"Great!" I said, feeling relieved. It wouldn't have been fair to take their llama and change his name without their permission.

"If we come back to Vermont to visit, we'll stop by your home to see how he's doing," said Mr. Lindsey, giving the brown llama a final hug.

Ira Allen was sitting with his knees folded under him, in the funny way that llamas often do, in the back of the truck. He was humming softly, just like Ethan Allen. Soon they could hum to each other. I would have liked to sit in the back and listen, but I decided to keep my father and April company up front.

Dad turned on the ignition of the truck, and we began to move slowly down their driveway.

"Wait. Wait," called Mr. Lindsey.

"Oh, no," I moaned. "They've changed their minds." The whole plan had been so perfect and

worked out so well. I should have known it couldn't really be true.

My father put his foot on the brake, and the truck stopped. Mr. Lindsey came running up to us. "Wait just a minute," he said. Then he ran over to their yellow Llama Xing sign and pulled it out of the dirt.

"You're going to need this," he said, handing it to me through the open window.

"Thanks," I said. I was thanking him for not changing his mind as much as I was thanking him for the sign.

Then we all waved good-bye again, and my father slowly drove off. What a fantastic surprise this was going to be for my mother. What a fantastic surprise this was going to be for Ethan Allen. Starting today we wouldn't have just one llama. Now there were two llamas in our family.

"Adam," my father said as we drove along. "I have a feeling that your mother won't mind waiting a bit longer for that new refrigerator."

"You mean . . . ," I began.

"Yeah," he said, nodding his head.

He didn't say anything more, but I knew what he meant. One of these days, very soon, there was going to be still another surprise coming to our house. And it would have two wheels and a pair of pedals!